H. H Warner

Songs of the Spindle & Legends of the Loom

H. H Warner

Songs of the Spindle & Legends of the Loom

ISBN/EAN: 9783337020217

Printed in Europe, USA, Canada, Australia, Japan

Cover: Foto ©Andreas Hilbeck / pixelio.de

More available books at **www.hansebooks.com**

...adale

Songs of the Spindle

&

Legends of the Loom

Selected & Arranged

BY

H. H. Warner.

With Illustrations by A. Tucker, H. H. Warner, & Edith Capper.

"And all the women that were wisehearted did spin with their hands, and brought that which they had spun, both blue and purple, and of scarlet and fine linen."—Ex. 35, 25.

"My days are swifter than a weaver's shuttle."—Job 7. 5.

LONDON

Published by N. J. POWELL & CO.

1889.

Printed by Whiting & Co., at "Beaufort House," 30 & 32, Sardinia Street,
Lincoln's Inn Fields, London, W.C.

To

Rev. S. A. Barnett & Mrs. Barnett,

𝔐𝔶 𝔉𝔯𝔦𝔢𝔫𝔡𝔰 𝔞𝔫𝔡 𝔥𝔢𝔩𝔭𝔢𝔯𝔰,

Who have done so much for workers in East London,
this Volume is affectionately dedicated.

Prefatory Note.

THIS little book is the product of *hand-work alone*, and we have chosen to produce it in this way because we wish to preserve in each copy, as much of that individuality and human interest, as the price at which it is offered will permit.

Not only was the paper made by hand, and the printing done by a hand-press, but the flax—which forms the basis of both Linen and Paper—was first spun by the cottagers at their wheels in the Langdale Valley, and the thread thus formed was afterwards specially woven for the cover of this book on the hand loom at the same place, which is shown so well on our frontispiece. The linen we have used for our cover is unbleached, and is therefore the natural colour of the dried flax. When the linen is required to be bleached, however, this is accomplished in Langdale, by no deleterious chemicals, but by the pure mountain air and sunshine—the only kind that the Bard of Avon knew when he sang of " the white sheet bleaching on the hedge" in the Daffodil-time.

Machines may well produce those necessities of life that require but little thought in their production, yet there is much that machinery can never accomplish. The very fact that a machine turns out thousands of a thing, each of which is alike in detail and finish, at once diminishes its art value. Machine-made goods, with all their superb mechanical finish, are monotonous in their uniformity, and lack that human touch, interest, and individuality for which the artistic mind craves.

It is, then, with pleasure that we are able to state that the illustration, printing, and binding of this little book are all the handiwork of English men and women. Further, as it is our conviction that a workman will not be so likely to put heart and soul into his labour, if the result of it is never to be known to the world as his, and as it is only right that honour should be given to whom honour is due, we have, as far as possible, *given the names* of all *craftsmen and workers* concerned in producing this volume, and we hope and believe that the purchasers of it will feel a kindly interest in knowing the names of those whose united handiwork they possess. For this idea we freely acknowledge we are in great measure indebted to " The Arts and Crafts Society."

The buyer of a thing may seldom think of the workers' sacrifice in producing it, yet the sacrifice of unremitting and often ill-rewarded toil should be thankfully acknowledged. And as sacrifice demands sacrifice, it is well to remember what John Ruskin has written, that the toiler can be best helped "by a right understanding on the part of all classes of what kinds of labour are good for men, raising them, and making them happy, by a determined sacrifice of such cheapness, convenience, and beauty, as is only to be got by the degradation of the workman, and by the equally determined demand for the products of healthy and ennobling labour."

If, then, in purchasing the finished article, the buyer be led to take an interest in the welfare of those concerned in producing it, and thus render the worker's sacrifice light and joyful, the purpose of these few words will have been accomplished.

H. H. WARNER.

The Names *of those who have assisted to produce*
this Book.

1. *Maker of Paper* ... ...
2. *Spinners of Thread* ... ... Eleanor Heskett, Martha Walker, and others.
3. *Weaver of Linen* ... ... John Thursby.
4. *Printer* ... ... Walter Thomson.
5. *Folder and Sewer* Sarah Coghlan and E. Marshall.
6. *Binder and Finisher* George Stockton & George Sims.
7. *Poets and Authors* Various, whose names are given at foot of selection
8. *Compiler and Editor* .. H. H. Warner.
9. *Illustrated by* ... ... Arthur Tucker, H. H. Warner, & Edith Capper.
10. *Reproduced by* The Autotype Company, John Swain.
11. *Ornamental Headings and Letters* F. Anderson.
12. *Published by* N. J. Powell & Co.

Contents.

Illustrations.

Forewords.

THE compiler of this little book has asked me to write a brief account of my effort to give back to a few of our Westmorland men and women " the venerable art torn from the poor." Within the covers of this little book are Spinning and Weaving songs stretching over a period of three thousand years, but the twin arts themselves go back to a still earlier period, as the illustrations overpage will show. The first given is the facsimile of a drawing found on an old Egyptian tomb, and shows the figures of two slaves spinning. In the British Museum, by the side of the rude spindles of which a sketch is given, there is preserved linen more than thirty centuries old, and to this day it remains unequalled for beauty of texture. In India, with the simplest appliances, they produced a linen so fine, that it was called "woven air." The figure of the girl spinning is drawn from a Greek vase, also in the British Museum. Through the art, the poetry, and the national life of a hundred races, the distaff held gentle sway, and the shuttle flew with rhythmic beat. In our own country, no maiden went to her new home without a "plenishing" of good linen, spun by her mother's and her own thrifty fingers. Then we come to the year 1787, when flax was

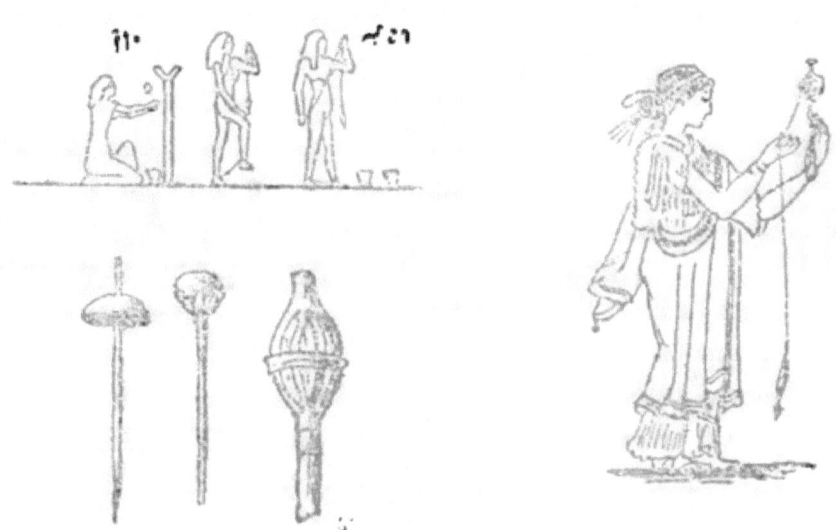

first spun by machinery, and ever since we have been devoting half our energies to inventing labour-saving machines, and the other half in discovering work for the unemployed.

As regards England, the good old handicrafts of spinning and weaving seemed finally dead and buried, and no man had ventured to write *Resurgam* on their tombstones. A few years ago, however, there was a wave of public feeling in the direction of reviving village industries, and a ripple of the great tide reached us here in Westmorland. I knew by experience that

> "It takes the ideal to blow an inch aside
> The dust of the actual,"

but, although I had many ideal incentives and suggestions, the practical difficulties were great, and I hesitated. At last, after long pondering over Wordsworth's sonnets and Mr. Ruskin's eloquent appeals in *Fors*, I was lifted into action by the homely speech of one of my poor neighbours. "When t'ould wheels died out," said she, "the gude times went too, m'happen they'd coome back if t'wheels did." Then I determined the wheels should come back. That was five years ago, and now all up and down Langdale, by many a quiet fireside, the murmur of the wheel is once more heard,

> "Soft as the dorhawk's to a distant ear."

Then I took a cottage and made it into a Spinning Home, routed out two looms and an old weaver, and set up a tidy bleaching ground, and here we spin, weave, and sell many hundred yards of honest, old-fashioned linen. It is interesting to know that the structure of the loom in use to-day is practically the same as that which Giotto represented on the Campanile. Every month-end the village women bring their yarn to the Spinning Home, where it is weighed, tested, and paid for. A good spinster can earn about six shillings a week spinning at odd hours by her fireside.

We produce a stout sheeting, pronounced by Mr. Ruskin to be "the soundest and fairest linen fabric that care can weave, or field dew blanch," and we spin and weave many different makes

for art needlework and decorative purposes, keeping a number of poor ladies employed embroidering approved designs on our linen.

During these past five years Langdale linen has been put to many wise and lovely purposes, but there seems a special grace and fitness in its being chosen to hold and bind together this little sheaf of spinning songs, gathered by kindly hands from long centuries of immortal verse.

ALBERT **FLEMING**.

Langdale, Ambleside.

THE UNRIPE FLAX.

" When through its half transparent stalk at eve
The level sunshine glimmers with green light."

COLERIDGE.

WHO can find a virtuous woman ?
  For her price is far above rubies,
  The heart of her husband can safely trust in her
  And he shall have no lack of gain.
She seeketh out the wool and flax,
And worketh willingly with her hands.
She layeth her hands to the distaff,
And her hands hold the spindle.
She is not afraid of the snow for her household ;
For all her household are clothed with double garments.
She maketh herself coverings of tapestry ;
Her clothing is fine linen and purple.
Her husband is known in the gates
When he sitteth among the elders of the land.
She maketh linen garments and selleth them,
And delivereth girdles unto the merchant.
Her children arise up and call her blessed ;
Her husband also, even he praiseth her.

Proverbs, Chap. 31.   שלמה (SOLOMON).

HEAR thou what device
    The God himself breathed in my soul, I reared
    Here in these halls a mighty loom of price,
    Anon before the suitors I appeared
And said, young men, my suitors, what I feared
Is come, divine Odysseus is no more;
Woo ye, but leave my widowhood revered,
Lest my long-purposed work fall void for ever more.

I for Laertes weave a funeral sheet
Against the final debt that he must pay,
And I were shamed the Achaian dames to meet
Should the long slumber find but shroudless clay
Of one who owned much lordship in his day.
So did I speak amid the suitor throng,
And so persuaded their proud hearts gave way.
Daily I weaved, and then, to work them wrong,
By night the woof unwound with torches ranged along.

Odyssey, Book xix.   Ὁμηρον (HOMER).

BOTH take their stations and the piece prepare,
And order ev'ry slender thread with care;
The web enwraps, the beam the reed divides,
While thro' the wid'ning space the shuttle glides
Which their swift hands receive; then poised with lead
The swinging weight strikes close th' inserted thread;
Each girds her flowing garments round her waist,
And plies her feet and arms with dextrous haste.

Metamorphoses, Book VI.   (OVID) PVBLIVS OVIDIVS NASO.

"The Trial of Arachne and the Goddess Pallas."

HE can spin,
    Then may I set the world on wheels
    When she can spin for her living.

Two Gentlemen of Verona.

The spinsters and the knitters in the sun,
And the free maids that weave
Their thread with bones
Do use to chant it; it is silly sooth,
And dallies with the innocence of love.   *Twelfth Night.*

When daffodils begin to peer—
    With heigh! the doxy over the dale,
Why, then comes in the sweet o' the year,
    For the red blood reigns in the winter's pale.

The white sheet bleaching on the hedge—
    With hey! the sweet birds, O how they sing,
Doth set my pugging tooth on edge;
    For a quart of ale is a dish for a king.   *Winter's Tale.*

I fear not Goliath with a weaver's beam,
Because I know also life is a shuttle.

The Merry Wives of Windsor.

I would I were a weaver,
I could sing Psalms or anything.   *Henry IV.*

Shakespeare.

20

" When daffodils begin to peer."

ERE we present a fleece
    To make a peece
      Of cloth,
    Nor faire, must you be loth
  Your fingers to apply
  To huswiferie,
  Then, then begin
    To spin ;
And sweetling, mark you,
  What a web will come
Into your chests drawn by your
  Painful thumb.
Set you to your wheele, and wax
Rich by ductile wool and fiax ;
Yarne is an income, and the huswives thread
The larder fils with meat, and bin with bread.

Hesperides.   𝕳errick.

AH! turn thine eyes
　　Where the poor homeless shivering female lies,
　　She once perhaps, in village plenty blest,
　　Has wept at tales of innocence distrest;
Her modest looks the cottage might adorn,
Sweet as the primrose peeps beneath the thorn;
Pinched with the cold, and shrinking from the shower,
With heavy heart deplores that luckless hour,
When idly first ambitious of the town,
She left her wheel and robes of country brown.

The Deserted Village.　　　　　　　　Goldsmith.

XCUSE is needless, when with love sincere
 Of occupation, not by fashion led,
 Thou turn'st the wheel that slept with dust o'erspread;
 My nerves from no such murmur shrink,—tho' near,
Soft as the Dorhawk's to a distant ear,
When twilight shades bedim the mountain's head.
She who was feigned to spin our vital thread
Might smile, O lady! on a task once dear
To household virtues. Venerable Art,
Torn from the poor! yet will kind Heaven protect
Its own, not left without a guiding chart,
If rulers, trusting with undue respect
To proud discoveries of Intellect,
Sanction the pillage of man's ancient heart.

𝔚𝔬𝔯𝔡𝔰𝔴𝔬𝔯𝔱𝔥.

SWIFTLY turn the murmuring wheel!
   Night has brought the welcome hour
  When the weary fingers feel
   Help as from a faëry power;
Dewy night o'ershades the ground;
Turn the swift wheel round and round!

Now beneath the starry sky
  Crouch the widely scattered sheep,—
Ply, the pleasant labour, ply!
  For the spindle, while they sleep,
Runs with motion smooth and fine,
Gathering up a trustier line.

Short-lived likings may be bred
  By a glance from fickle eyes;
But true love is like the thread
  Which the kindly wool supplies,
When the flocks are all at rest,
Sleeping on the mountain's breast.

                   Wordsworth.

" When the flocks are all at rest."

HEIR leader was false Sextus
    That wrought the deed of shame,
    With restless pace and haggard face
    To his last field he came.
Men said he saw strange visions
    Which none beside might see,
And that strange sounds were in his ears
    Which none might hear but he;
A woman fair and stately,
    But pale as are the dead,
Oft thro' the watches of the night
    Sat spinning by his bed;
And as she plied the distaff,
    In a sweet voice and low,
She sang of great old houses,
    And fights fought long ago.
So spun she, and so sang she,
    Until the east was grey,
Then pointed to her bleeding breast,
    And shrieked and fled away.   Macaulay.

O he entered the house: and the hum of the wheel and the singing
Suddenly ceased ; for Priscilla, aroused by his step on the threshold,
Rose as he entered, and gave him her hand, in signal of welcome,
Saying—"I knew it was you, when I heard your step in the passage ;
For I was thinking of you, as I sat there singing and spinning."
Awkward and dumb with delight, that a thought of him had been mingled
Thus in the sacred psalm, that came from the heart of the maiden,
Silent before her he stood, and gave her the flowers for an answer,
Finding no words for his thought.

Longfellow.

The hum of the wheel and the singing suddenly ceased.

O as she sat at her wheel one afternoon in Autumn,
Alden, who opposite sat, and was watching her
dexterous fingers,
As if the thread she was spinning were that of his
life and his fortune,
After a pause in their talk, thus spake to the sound of the spindle.
"Truly, Priscilla," he said, "when I see you spinning and spinning,
Never idle a moment, but thrifty and thoughtful of others,
Suddenly you are transformed, are visibly changed in a moment;
You are no longer Priscilla, but Bertha the Beautiful Spinner."
Here the light foot on the treadle grew swifter and swifter; the
spindle
Uttered an angry snarl, and the thread snapped short in her fingers;
While the impetuous speaker, not heeding the mischief, con-
tinued—
"You are the beautiful Bertha, the spinner, the queen of
Helvetia;
She whose story I read at a stall in the streets of Southampton,
Who, as she rode on her palfrey, o'er valley, and meadow, and
mountain
Ever was spinning her thread from a distaff fixed to her saddle."

Longfellow.

27

COFT a stave o' haslock **woo'**
To make a **coat to** Johnny o't,
For Johnny is my only Jo',
I lo'e him best of **ony yet.**
The cardin' o't, the spinnin' o't,
The warpin' o't, the winnin' o't,
When ilka ell cost me a groat,
The tailor stole the lynin' o't.

For tho' his locks be lyart gray,
And tho' his brow be beld aboon,
Yet I hae seen him on a day
The pride of a' the parish in.
The cardin' o't, the spinnin' o't,
The warpin' o't, the winnin' o't,
When ilka ell cost me a groat,
The tailor stole the lynin' o't.

Burns.

28

An auld Irish wheel wid a young Irish girl at it.

HOW me a sight,
    Bates for delight,
      An ould Irish wheel wid a young
          Irish girl at it.

O! no!
Nothin' you'll show
Aquals her sittin' and takin' a twirl at it.

Look at her there,
Night in her hair—
The blue ray of day from her eye
      Laughin' out on us!
    Faix, an' a foot
    Perfect of cut,
Peepin' to put an end to all
      Doubt in us.

See! the lambs' wool
'Turns coarse an' dull
By them soft, beautiful,
      Weeshy, white hands of her.
    Down goes her heel,
    Round runs the wheel,
Purrin' wid pleasure to take
      The commands of her.

   A. P. Graves

THE SPINDLE, THE SHUTTLE, AND THE NEEDLE.

A Fairy Tale.

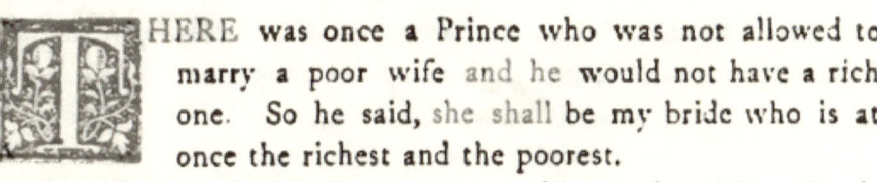

HERE was once a Prince who was not allowed to marry a poor wife and he would not have a rich one. So he said, she shall be my bride who is at once the richest and the poorest.

And it chanced that he came to a village where there dwelt a poor maiden, and looking thro' the cottage window, he saw how industriously she was engaged at her spinning wheel. She looked up, and as soon as she saw the prince looking at her, she blushed as red as a rose, and looked down again, industriously turning her wheel round.

Whether the thread was even or not just then, I know not, but she spun on till the prince rode away. Then she stepped to the window and opened it, saying, "Oh, how hot this room is!" but she remained there till she could no longer see the white feathers in the prince's hat.

The Spindle, the Shuttle, & the Needle.

When she sat down at her work again, she remembered some-
thing that her godmother used to repeat. And she sang

> "Spindle, spindle, out with you,
> And bring a wooer home."

Scarcely had she done so when the spindle sprang from her
hands and merrily danced away over the fields, leaving a golden
thread behind it. Then having no spindle, the maiden took the
shuttle into her hands and began to weave. Meanwhile the
spindle danced on till it reached the king's son, and it turned
the horse's head, and he rode back, guided by the golden thread.
At the same time the girl sitting at work sang

> "Shuttle, shuttle, out with you,
> And bring a wooer home."

Immediately it sprang out of her hands and through the door,
and before this it began to weave a more beautiful pattern than
ever before known, which seemed to grow of itself.

Then, because the shuttle had flown away, the maiden sat
down to sew, and sang as she stitched:

> "Needle, needle, sharp and fine,
> Fit the house for wooer mine."

And the needle flew from her fingers, and it seemed as if invisible
hands were at work, for in a few minutes the table was covered
with a cloth, the chairs with velvet, and on the walls hung silken
curtains. And scarcely had the needle put in the last stitch when

the maiden saw again the prince's white plumes as he came to the cottage, drawn by the golden thread of the spindle.

And entering, the prince said, "Come with me and be my bride, for you are both the poorest yet the richest maiden," and she said nothing, but held out her hand, which the prince took, and he gave her a kiss and seated her on his horse, and led her to the king's castle, where they were wedded.

And the spindle, the shuttle, and the needle were placed in the treasure chamber.

Surely he who possesses a thrifty and industrious wife, though she be poor, yet is she rich, and maketh her husband rich also.

A Fairy Tale from Grimm's Collection.